# Thank You, Brother Bear

Story by **HANS BAUMANN** Pictures by **ERIC CARLE**

**SCHOLASTIC INC.**

New York Toronto London Auckland Sydney

# Long ago and far away to the north,

where even the great sea freezes to solid ice in the winter's cold, there lived three brothers named Strong Bow, Shining Spear and Chip. Strong Bow and Shining Spear were older than Chip, and they were great hunters. But Chip loved the animals of the forest too much to hurt them.

The three brothers lived in a small wooden house deep in the woods with Nuni, their grandmother, and Bright Sun, their little sister. Their parents weren't alive anymore.

Whenever Strong Bow and Shining Spear went hunting, Chip stayed at home. Then, when they were far away, Chip would call to his other brothers, the ones nobody knew about: Bear, Beaver and Moose. "Now it is safe for you to come out," he would tell them.

One day in the autumn, as the cold winds began to blow, Strong Bow and Shining Spear said to Chip, "We must go hunting for our winter's food. We will be gone many days this time. Be sure you take good care of our little sister."
"Oh, I'll be all right," said Bright Sun, smiling her pretty smile.

But one day Bright Sun stopped smiling. She was ill. Grand-mother Nuni tried all the remedies she knew, but still Bright Sun grew sicker. Finally Nuni said to Chip, "Only Wise Raven has the medicine that can cure her. But between our house and his are the wild river, the wide swamp, the high mountain and the cold, deep lake. How can we possibly get to Wise Raven? What can we do? You are just a little boy — too young for such a long, dangerous journey."

I will do it! thought Chip, but he said nothing. And when Grandmother Nuni was not looking, Chip slipped silently out of the house.

Chip walked through the forest until he came to the bank of the wild river. Grandmother was right, he thought. I cannot cross this river. But if I don't, what will happen to Bright Sun? Just then, Beaver came by. "Don't worry, Chip," said Beaver. "I'll help you." Quickly Beaver chopped down a tree to make a bridge, and Chip hurried across the bridge to the other side of the wild river. "Thank you, Brother Beaver," said Chip.

But there on the other side of the wild river Chip found a wide, muddy swamp. I can never get across the swamp, he thought. Grandmother was right. But just then Moose came by and said, "I will help you."
And Moose carried Chip across the wide, muddy swamp.
"Thank you, Brother Moose," said Chip.

At the other side of the swamp, however, Chip saw a tall, tall mountain, like a huge wall of rocks. Grandmother was right, thought Chip. No one could get over this mountain. But just then Bear came by, and said, "I will help you. Just get on my back." With Chip on his back, Bear climbed right over the mountain. "Thank you, Brother Bear," said Chip.

But now, Chip found himself at the shore of a wide, deep lake. Chip put his hand into the lake. It was cold as ice. At the other side, he could see the hut in which Wise Raven lived. Well, Grandmother was right, thought Chip. I could never get across this wide, deep lake. But just then a huge black bird appeared and called to him, "Follow me." The bird flew out over the water.

To Chip's surprise, he found himself changed to a fish. In his new form he was able to swim across the wide, cold lake quite easily. When he reached the other side, he saw the big black bird fly into the hut where Wise Raven lived. Then out of the hut came Wise Raven himself. He covered Chip in a warm blanket, for Chip was no longer a fish, but was again a little boy, and he was feeling very cold. When Chip explained that Bright Sun was ill, Wise Raven gave him the special medicine she needed and rowed Chip back across the lake. "Thank you, Wise Raven" said Chip. "Now I must take the medicine back to my little sister."

At the foot of the mountain, Brother Bear was waiting for him, to help him on his way home. At the swamp stood Brother Moose. And Brother Beaver helped him back across the wild river.

"Where have you been? I have been worried about you," scolded Grandmother Nuni when Chip got back home again. Instead of answering her, Chip handed her the medicine for Bright Sun.

After a few days, Bear, Beaver and Moose came to the wooden house to inquire about Bright Sun's health. "Thank you, Brother Bear, Brother Beaver and Brother Moose," said Bright Sun, smiling. "I am perfectly well again." Just at this moment the hunters came back. Their sacks were loaded with game; no one would go hungry that winter. Shining Spear and Strong Bow pointed at Bear, Beaver and Moose. "Who are these strangers?" they asked.

Bright Sun said, "They are not strangers, they are Chip's other brothers." "What do you mean?" asked Strong Bow and Shining Spear. "*We* are Chip's only brothers."

"Chip has many brothers," said Nuni, the grandmother. "Come inside, have something to eat, and listen — I will tell you a story." She smiled at them and began, "Long ago and far away to the north, where even the great sea freezes to solid ice in the winter's cold, there lived three brothers..."

ISBN 0-590-25487-1

First published in the U.S.A. by Philomel Books, a division of The Putnam Publishing Group.

Text copyright © 1985 by Philomel Books, a division of The Putnam Publishing Group.
Illustrations copyright © 1983 by Eric Carle.
All rights reserved. Published by Scholastic Inc.
BLUE RIBBON is a registered trademark of Scholastic Inc.

12 11 10 9 8 7 6 5 4 3 2 1          5 6 7 8 9/9 0/0

Printed in the U.S.A.                    08

First Scholastic printing, January 1995
Originally published as: *Chip Has Many Brothers*.
Translation of: *Tschip hat viele Brüder*.

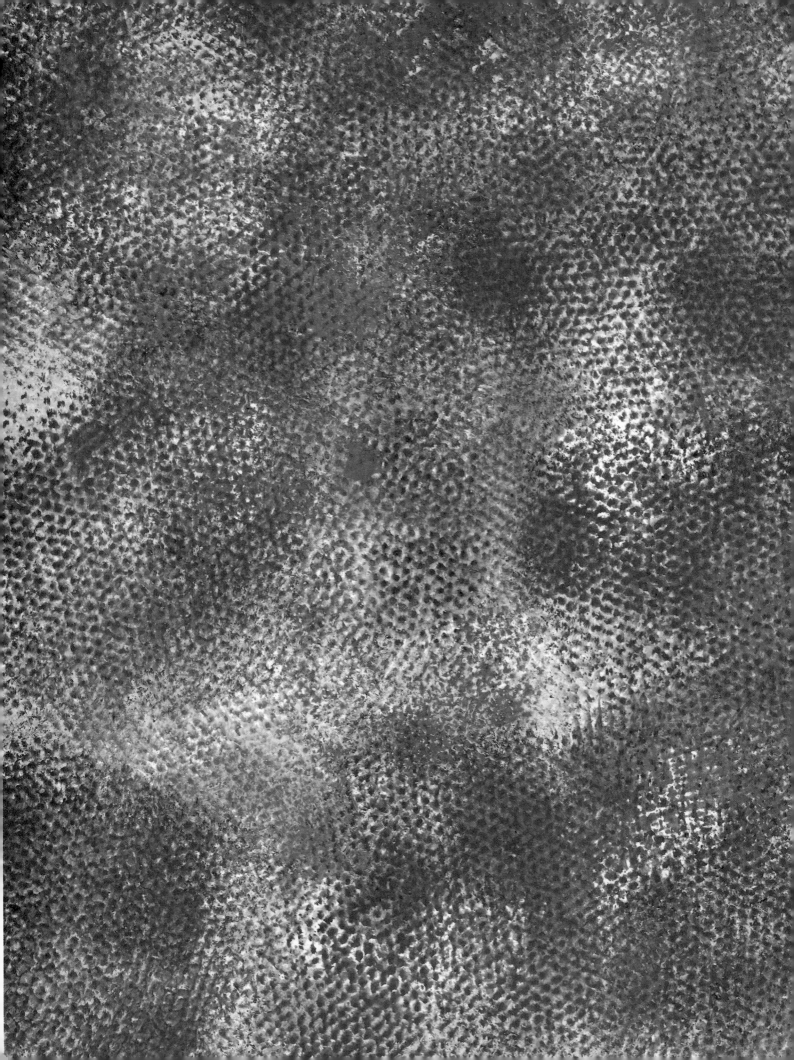